Be Like A Pineapple

By: Allyson Carter

DEDICATION

I would like to dedicate this book to…anyone that has big hopes and dreams, never give up!

- Allyson Carter

This is Confident Pineapple. All pineapples follow this quote…

"Stand Tall, Wear a Crown and Be Sweet on the Inside."

- Kathrin Gaskin

What does it mean to "Stand Tall?"
Well the pineapples stand up for themselves and anyone else that needs it.

What does it mean to "Wear a Crown?"
Well the pineapples wear the green crown on their heads and this helps them know they can have confidence.

What does it mean to "Be Sweet on the Inside?"
Well the pineapples outside is tough and the inside is sweet, so this means that pineapples know to be kind but also have thick skin.

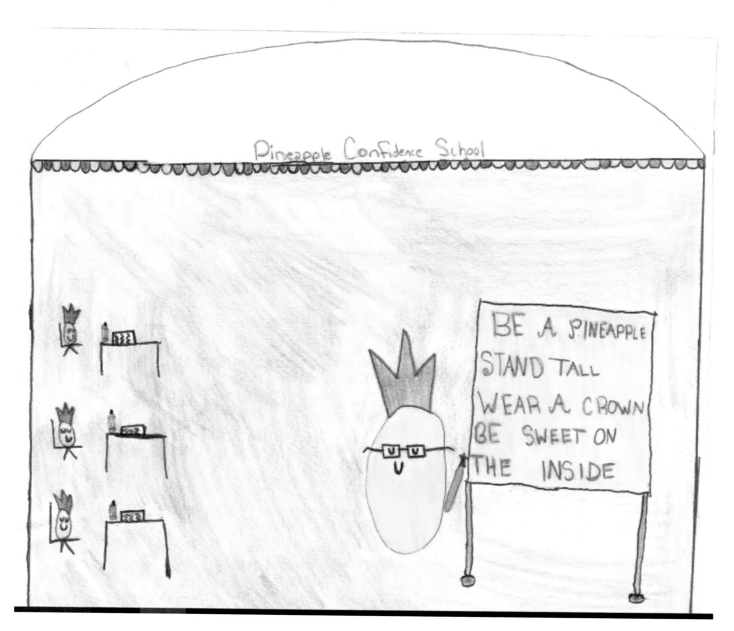

Once in the Produce market the pineapples noticed a group of Rotten Fruits. The Pitless Avocado, the Bruised Apple and the Seedless Strawberry who did not know the ways of the pineapples **yet**…

Pitless Avocado, Bruised Apple and Seedless Strawberry did not know how to "Stand Tall, Wear A Crown and Be Sweet On the Inside.

Pitless Avocado never stood up for himself or others.

Bruised Apple was always jealous of the other Apples beautiful skin.

Seedless Strawberry was never invited to the annual Strawberry family games.

Confident Pineapple wanted to teach the Rotten Fruits the "Ways of the Pineapple." Confident Pineapple gathered all of the other Pineapples to help the Rotten Fruits become Confident and not so rotten.

So, Confident Pineapple led all the other Pineapples on an adventure to the "Rotten Side of the Grocery Market." They all jumped into a shopping cart that a person shopping was carrying and jumped out just in time to the case of The Pitless Avocado, The Bruised Apple and The Seedless Strawberry.

Confident Pineapple says hi to the rotten group of fruits and introduces him and the other pineapples to them. Confident Pineapple asks the rotten fruits...

"Why are you guys so sad, angry or even mad every day?"

And the Pitless Avocado responds by saying...

"We each don't have the one thing that helps us fit in to the normal fruit that we are supposed to be. Like I'm an Avocado but I have no pit. I guess I'll never know what it's like to have a pit."

After Confident Pineapple spoke with Pitless Avocado he decided to talk with Bruised Apple…

"Well hi their Bruised Apple I am Confident Pineapple! My friends and I traveled over this way to help you learn the Pineapple Ways! We were confused why you guys act so sad all the time?" -Said Confident Pineapple

"Hello. Well we all are the unwanted fruits because of what we don't have or what we look like. For me I am bruised and that's why people think I look weird or gross. I guess I'll never know what it's like to have beautiful clear skin."
-Said Bruised Apple

Lastly Confident Pineapple wanted to talk with Seedless Strawberry about why the fruits over this way are so sad and rotten all the time…

"Hello their Seedless Strawberry, I am Confident Pineapple, after talking with some of your friends I wanted to ask you the same thing. Well, my Pineapple friends and I were worried and confused why you guys are so rotten?"

Seedless Strawberry replied by saying…

"Hi, we are unfortunately the rotten fruits. Along with that means we are shy, nervous and never invited to our family fruit games. I guess I'll never know what it's like to have seeds."

Confident Pineapple speaks to each of the Rotten Fruits to help them become less Rotten and more Confident in their Flaws.

Pitless Avocado, you do not need a pit to feel normal or to be able to stick up for yourself! You are beautiful just the way you are!

Bruised Apple, you do not need beautiful clear skin to feel beautiful! All that matters are the inside not the outside! You are beautiful just the way you are!

Seedless Strawberry, you do not need seeds to be invited to your Fruit Family Games or to ever feel confident! You are beautiful just the way you are!

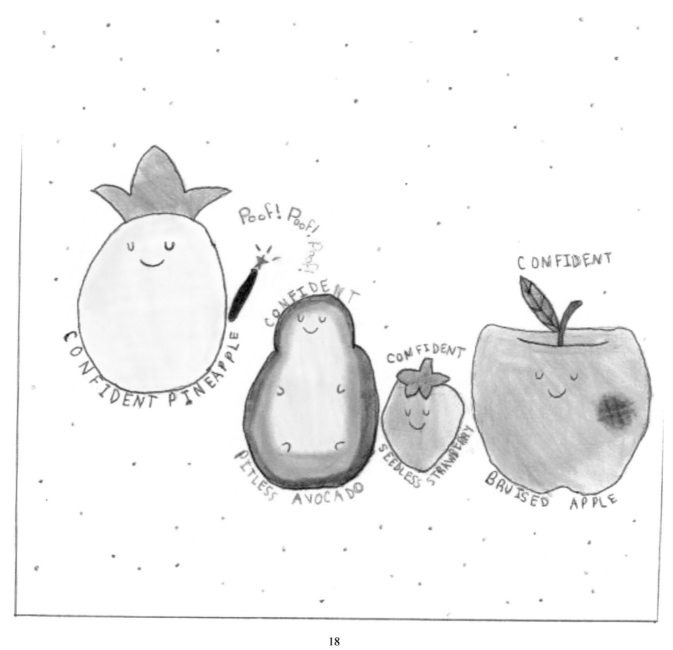

The group of Rotten Fruits thanked Confident Pineapple along with his other Pineapple friends for coming to help them be like a pineapple

"Wow I guess us Rotten Fruits don't really need to be so Rotten." -Says Pitless Avocado

"Yeah Pitless Avocado let's be confident like the Confident Pineapple and his friends." -Says Bruised Apple

"Let's all just be like a Pineapple; we can all Stand Tall, Wear a Crown and Be Sweet on the Inside! -Says Seedless Strawberry

After this monumental moment in the Produce Market Pitless Avocado, Bruised Apple and Seedless Strawberry started to become more and more positive and less rotten every day.

The Pitless Avocado, Bruised Apple and Seedless Strawberry joined the "Confident Side of the Produce Market."

And the group of the Pitless Avocado, Bruised Apple and Seedless Strawberry decided to teach the rest of the fruits in the Produce Market how to be like a Pineapple

And in the end the Pitless Avocado, Bruised Apple and Seedless Strawberry want to teach you how to Be Like A Pineapple…

1. Stand Tall
2. Wear A Crown
3. Be Sweet On the Inside

You Can Do It!!!

ABOUT ME!

Hello, I am Allyson Carter the writer and illustrator of "Be Like A Pineapple". This idea and quote have really shaped me into who I am today. I am a Sophomore in High School and I just completed my first year of Varsity Cross Country and I play Travel Softball. I have a brother Robbie who's in the seventh grade and we own a Valley Bull Dog "Sweetie", she is a mix of a Boxer and Old English Bull Dog.

Shout out to Mom and Dad, thank you for always believing in me!